Sense Pass King

A STORY FROM CAMEROON

retold by

KATRIN TCHANA

illustrated by

TRINA SCHART HYMAN

HOLIDAY HOUSE / New York

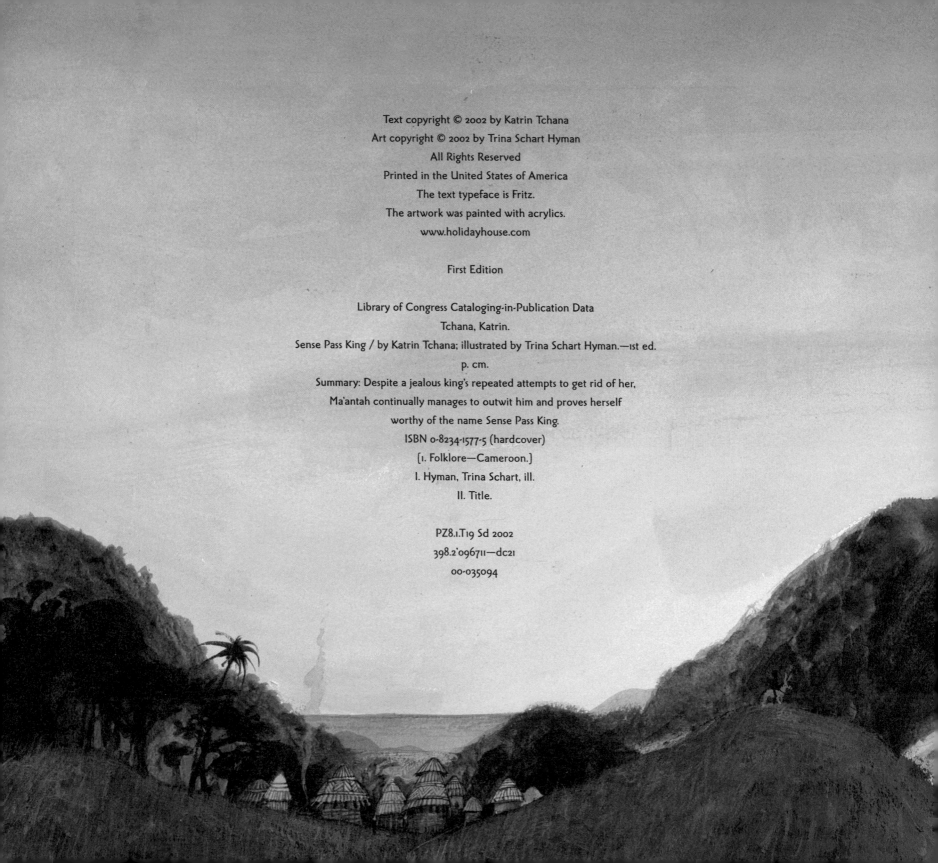

Printed in the United States of America
The text typeface is Fritz.
The artwork was painted with acrylics.
www.holidayhouse.com

First Edition

Library of Congress Cataloging-in-Publication Data
Tchana, Katrin.
Sense Pass King / by Katrin Tchana; illustrated by Trina Schart Hyman.—1st ed.
p. cm.
Summary: Despite a jealous king's repeated attempts to get rid of her,
Ma'antah continually manages to outwit him and proves herself
worthy of the name Sense Pass King.
ISBN 0-8234-1577-5 (hardcover)
[1. Folklore—Cameroon.]
I. Hyman, Trina Schart, ill.
II. Title.

PZ8.1.T19 Sd 2002
398.2'096711—dc21
00-035094

For Eugene
—K. T.

For Lloyd Alexander
and for Xavier
—T. S. H.

IN THE LAND OF SEVEN VILLAGES lived a man and a woman.
They were simple farmers and happy enough, except that they had no children.
Then at last the woman gave birth to a baby girl and named her Ma'antah.

It soon became clear that Ma'antah was an exceptional child. Before she was
one year old she could walk and talk.

By the time she was two she could speak the languages of all seven villages and communicate with animals. When she was three, she could prepare dinner for her parents. The villagers were amazed by Ma'antah's cleverness. Soon they began to call her Sense Pass King, because she had more sense than even the king.

It wasn't long before news of this child reached the king himself.

"How can this be?" he wondered. "A little girl, not even four years old. Outrageous!"

"Go and find the child Ma'antah," he told his soldiers. "The one the stupid villagers call Sense Pass King. Take her to the heart of the forest and leave her there. The panthers and the snakes will take care of her."

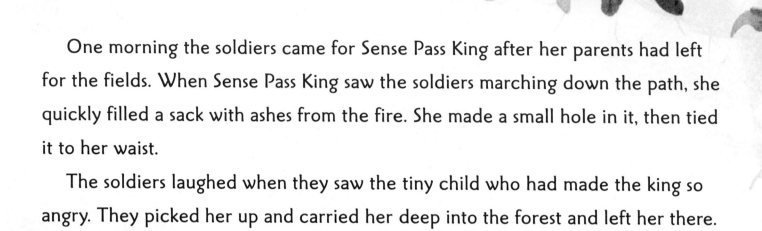

One morning the soldiers came for Sense Pass King after her parents had left for the fields. When Sense Pass King saw the soldiers marching down the path, she quickly filled a sack with ashes from the fire. She made a small hole in it, then tied it to her waist.

The soldiers laughed when they saw the tiny child who had made the king so angry. They picked her up and carried her deep into the forest and left her there. As soon as they had gone, Sense Pass King followed the trail of ashes that had trickled through the hole in the sack. In no time at all she was safely home again.

The years passed. Sense Pass King became more intelligent each day. She thought of better ways for the farmers to plant their crops. Soon the farmers were growing twice as many vegetables. Next she invented a machete that allowed the villagers to clear their fields in half the time it had once taken them.

Sense Pass King became very popular. People came to ask her for advice whenever they had a problem.

The king began hearing rumors that Sense Pass King was still alive. He was furious and decided to get rid of her once and for all. He instructed his soldiers to dig a pit behind the palace. He would trap Sense Pass King there until she starved to death.

As soon as Sense Pass King heard that soldiers were digging a pit, she guessed the king's plan. That night, while her parents slept, she went outside and asked her friends the moles to do her a favor.

In a few days the soldiers came to take Sense Pass King away. Her mother and
father began to cry, but Ma'antah went without a fuss. After the soldiers put her in the
pit, she found the entrance to the tunnel the moles had dug and crawled back to
her house.

When the king found that Sense Pass King had escaped his trap, he was shaken. The young girl must be extraordinarily powerful, he thought to himself. Better to keep her near me, where I can watch her every move. He ordered Ma'antah to come live with him in the palace. There he kept her busy washing clothes and pounding grain.

Every evening after the day's work was finished, the king called Ma'antah to bring him his pipe. While he sat by his fire smoking, he talked to himself about the problems in his kingdom. Ma'antah stayed quietly beside him. After the king finished speaking, she gave him suggestions. The king took her good advice, and the people of the seven villages were happy and prosperous.

One day a messenger came to the kingdom. "A powerful emperor in a faraway country wishes to give his daughter in marriage to the suitor he finds most worthy," he said. The king was overjoyed. A marriage to the emperor's daughter would increase his wealth and influence, he decided. He prepared to journey to the emperor's court.

The king took ten of his most trusted soldiers and Ma'antah to cook for them. The party traveled for three days and three nights across the ocean.

The emperor greeted the king and his company. He called for his daughter, Titayah, to come and meet the strangers. Although she was still a child, she was already as beautiful as the evening star.

The king was pleased at the thought of marrying this lovely creature. "Your Excellency," he addressed the emperor, "I assure you that I will care for your daughter as I would a precious jewel."

"Perhaps," replied the emperor. "But she's still a child. It will be years before she's ready for marriage. If you think you can care for her, prove it to me.

"Ever since birth, Titayah has had a very poor appetite. If you want to take my daughter, prove that you will make her eat properly."

The king ordered Ma'antah to prepare a delicious meal for Titayah. She cooked rice and chicken, meat and soup, cakes and vegetables. She gathered mangoes and bananas and coconuts and peanuts. When the meal was ready, the king called for Titayah.

"See all the delicious food I've prepared for you?" the king asked the little girl. "Go ahead and eat!"

But Titayah only shrugged. "I'm not hungry," she said.

"Titayah, wait," called Ma'antah. "I want to show you something." Ma'antah untied a string of bells from around her waist and began to play a song.

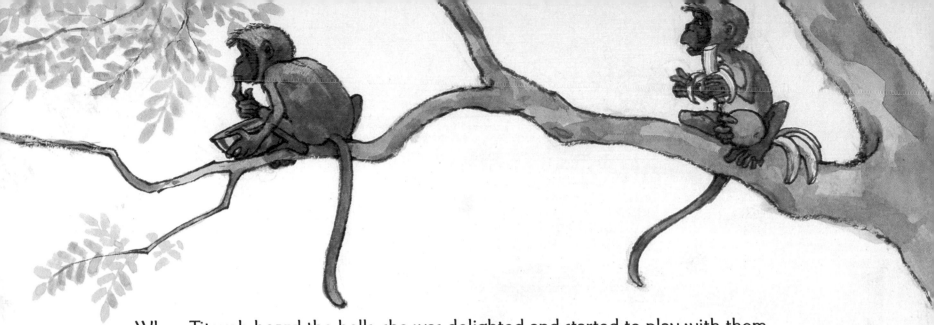

When Titayah heard the bells, she was delighted and started to play with them. She opened her mouth in laughter, and Ma'antah quickly popped in a small piece of mango. The little princess was so happy with the bells, she chewed and swallowed without thinking about it. Then Sense Pass King fed her a piece of chicken, all the while continuing the game with the bells. In this way Titayah soon finished the meal.

The emperor smiled at Ma'antah. "You are a very clever young woman. I entrust my daughter to *your* care."

The enraged king held up his machete to kill Sense Pass King then and there.

"Wait, Your Majesty," she whispered to him. "Don't shame yourself before the emperor. Remember, I live in the palace with you. Everything I own is yours, even the little princess. When Titayah is old enough, she'll marry you, just as you planned."

The king saw the truth in Ma'antah's words. He agreed to let Ma'antah bring the little girl home.

As they left the emperor's lands, all was calm. But as soon as they were out to sea, the ship was almost capsized by an enormous wave. From behind the wave a horrible sea lizard rose. He was bigger than a baobab tree and had seven heads. Each of his seven mouths spouted fire and steam.

"Where is the princess?" the monster thundered. "Give me the princess!"

The soldiers tried to shoot the monster, but their arrows bounced off his thick scales.

"Shoot his eyes!" cried Sense Pass King. But the dreadful creature terrified the men so that their hands shook, and most of the arrows missed. Soon there was only one arrow left, but the monster still had four heads.

"What shall we do?" the soldiers asked their king.

"Give him the princess," he cried, shaking with fear. "We have to save ourselves."

Sense Pass King couldn't let that happen. "Hand me your bow," she ordered the soldier with one last arrow. "I can kill him."

The king spat at her. "You? What can you do?" But the soldier handed the bow to Sense Pass King.

Standing in front of the sea lizard with the bow hidden behind her, Sense Pass King suddenly began to scream. "Oh no, oh no, first you came, and now you've brought your brother, too. What will happen to us now?"

When the monster heard this, he was very surprised. He thought he was the only one of his kind. He looked left and right, his heads swiveling in every direction, trying to catch a glimpse of his brother.

"Don't you see him?" cried Sense Pass King, pointing to the right. "He's over there, even bigger than you. Oh no, oh no!"

The monster craned all four of his remaining heads in the direction Sense Pass King pointed. As soon as his eyes were looking in the same direction, Ma'antah raised her bow and aimed. Her single arrow passed through all his eight eyes. With flames bellowing from his dreadful mouths, the monster sank to the bottom of the sea.

The travelers returned to the seven villages with the beautiful Titayah. All the people came out to welcome them and hear the story of their journey. The king told everyone he had won the child for his bride, and had rescued the ship from the terrible sea lizard. But his soldiers, disgusted by his cowardice and dishonesty, told the people the truth, that they owed their lives to the bravery and wisdom of Sense Pass King.

That is how Sense Pass King lost her name. When the people heard the true story, they drove the king from the palace and away from the seven villages. Then they made Ma'antah their queen.

Queen Ma'antah ruled wisely and well. She taught Titayah how to speak the language of the animals. The little princess befriended the wild creatures of the forest, who often came to visit the palace. The people of the seven villages lived in peace and prosperity for all the years of Ma'antah's reign.

Note from the Author

I first heard the story "Sense Pass King" from my husband. He heard it from his mother when he was a little boy growing up in the West African nation of Cameroon. It is a story told by the people who live in the Northwest province of Cameroon. Although today Cameroon is a republic with a president, the people of the Northwest province still honor their traditional kings, who play an important part in local government and live in beautiful palaces.

In the story my husband told me, Sense Pass King is a little boy, not a little girl. When I retold the story, I decided to make Sense Pass King a girl, because we already know many stories about brave and clever little boys but not so many about brave and clever little girls. Historically, there have been powerful queens in Africa, but as far as I know there has never been a ruling queen in Cameroon.

Sense Pass King means "smarter than the king" in Pidgin English, which is a dialect of English spoken in northwest Cameroon. It evolved when the local people adapted the English language to suit their own culture and needs. Pidgin English uses many of the same words as the English most Americans speak, but the words are put together in different ways, so it's almost like a separate language.